Flamingo Sunset

by
Jonathan London

illustrated by
Kristina Rodanas

Marshall Cavendish Children

As the spring sun sinks
into the tropical sea,
two flamingos
build a cone-shaped mud nest
at the water's edge.

Then the female
lays a single white egg.

For thirty days,
the two mates take turns
keeping their egg warm.

For thirty days,
something grows
inside the precious egg.

Then a peck
and a crack,
and a tiny bill pokes out . . .

and a sticky wet head.

Finally a whole wobbly chick stands . . . falls down . . . stands again, and makes a squeaky, puppy-like bark.

The chick is hungry.

Mother Flamingo
drips red, fat-rich crop "milk"
down into the chick's wide-open mouth.

At a week old,
the baby waddles on wobbly legs
down to the edge of the salt lagoon
and watches Mother and Father feed.

Wading along, they scoop water
and brine shrimp into their long bills,
skimming the surface.

The chick wants to try too.
He steps on dainty feet—
and snags a tiny insect!

A few weeks later, an eerie silence
settles over the pink city of flamingos.
Standing on one leg, heads tucked beneath
wings, they wait.

Suddenly, their snake-like necks shoot up—and the whole colony honks a loud alarm.

Black clouds flash with jagged fire.
Thunder booms like surf.
A storm is coming!

The chick scuttles to his mother.
His father huddles close.
The sky cracks open like a giant egg . . .

and the rain crashes down.
Palms whip and bend
in the roaring wind . . .

and lightning rips the sky!

The next morning,
the sun bursts out
and fills the world with light.

The chick shakes his soft, downy feathers and spreads his fragile wings to dry. The storm is over. The day is bright.

Months come and go.
The chick grows and grows.
His elegant, pink plumes come in.
It's almost time now . . .

time to fly!

Finally, the day has come!
He will go on his first feeding trip!
Along with his mother and father,
and the rest of the huge flock,

the young bird runs on water,
flapping his wings,
and lifts off—neck stretched forward,
legs floating behind—gracefully flying . . .

. . . into a flaming, flamingo sunset.

Next year, the flamingos will be back—
building mud nests
at the water's edge . . .

and laying in each one
a precious white egg.

Author's Note

Flamingos live in huge flocks, sometimes containing more than ten thousand birds. They mate in the spring and early summer. The male and female stay together for life.

For twenty-eight to thirty-one days, the parents take turns sitting on the single white egg. Once the chick is born, the parents feed it for four to five weeks. Flamingos are filter feeders. They scoop food and water into their bills with their heads skimming upside down. The tongue pumps water through bristles that line the bill, like those of a baleen whale. The flamingo feeds on small insects, brine shrimp, and tiny clams.

After seventy to seventy-five days, a young flamingo's feathers have all grown in. Then it can fly! Many flamingos migrate once a year, but some species go on feeding trips instead.

A chick's natural enemies include eagles, sea gulls, and hawks. But a flamingo's greatest enemy is man. In the nineteenth century, flamingos in Florida were hunted for their plumage. Now, due to the loss of their natural habitat, flamingos no longer nest anywhere in the United States. The flamingos in this book are the "greater flamingos" of Bonaire, an island in the Caribbean. Conservation is the only hope for the future of these magnificent, graceful birds—among the most beautiful in all creation.

For Claire—pretty in pink,
and for sweet Maureen, my research assistant
—J.L.

For Arthur who gave me wings
—K.R.

Text copyright © 2008 by Jonathan London
Illustrations copyright © 2008 by Kristina Rodanas
All rights reserved
Marshall Cavendish Corporation
99 White Plains Road, Tarrytown, NY 10591
www.marshallcavendish.us/kids
Library of Congress Cataloging-in-Publication Data
London, Jonathan, 1947–
Flamingo sunset / by Jonathan London ; illustrated by Kristina Rodanas. — 1st ed.
p. cm.
ISBN 978-0-7614-5384-0
1. Flamingos—Juvenile literature. I. Rodanas, Kristina, ill. II. Title.
QL696.C56L56 2008
598.3'5—dc22
2007013763

The text of this book is set in Century Schoolbook.
The illustrations are rendered in color pencil over watercolor wash.

Book design by Vera Soki
Editor: Margery Cuyler

Printed in China
First edition
1 3 5 6 4 2

mc **Marshall Cavendish**
Children